Slam Dunk Series

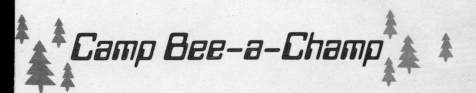

Camp Bee-a-Champ

Tess Eileen Kindig
Illustrated by Joe VanSeveren

SAINT LOUIS

For the entire Bean family who shared camp stories and let me come to lunch and be part of the reunion! Fun day —thanks.

Slam Dunk Series

Sixth Man Switch

Spider McGhee and the Hoopla

Zip, Zero, Zilch

Muggsy Makes an Assist

Gimme an "A"!

March Mania

Double Whammy!

Camp Bee-a-Champ

Copyright © 2001 Tess Eileen Kindig
Published by Concordia Publishing House
3558 S. Jefferson Avenue, St. Louis, MO 63118-3968
Manufactured in the United States of America

Library of Congress Cataloging-in-Publication Data
Kindig, Tess Eileen.
    Camp Bee-a-Champ / Tess Eileen Kindig.
      p. cm. -- (Slam dunk series)
    Summary: While spending a week at basketball camp, fifth grader Mickey asks God for help when he worries about his playing ability, his grandmother's deteriorating health, and a mysterious ghost.
    ISBN 0-570-07143-7
    [1. Camps--Fiction. 2. Basketball--Fiction. 3. Christian life--Fiction.] I. Title.
    PZ7.K5663 Cam 2001
    [Fic]--dc21   00-011742

1 2 3 4 5 6 7 8 9 10   10 09 08 07 06 05 04 03 02 01

Slam Dunk Series

Contents

A Pink and
Purple Problem

"It's here! It's here!" my best friend, Zack Zeno, shouted, yanking the sleeve of my T-shirt.

My heart did a jump shot as the big yellow bus lumbered into the rec center parking lot. I flew up off my dad's old Army duffel bag and danced around like a maniac. It was really-and-truly-honest-to-Pete happening—we were on our way to basketball camp!

"Mickey, people are looking at you," my little sister, Meggie, said. About 14 times louder than she had to.

Who cared? Let 'em look. Last year I hadn't been able to afford basketball camp, and this year I was going—thanks to Zack's dad and his new wife Jo. They paid my way as a thank-you gift to my family for keeping Zack at our house for four months while Mr. Zeno worked for the railroad, first in Minnesota and then in Wisconsin.

"Somebody pinch me!" Zack shouted. "This can't be for real!"

Our new friend, Walker Adams, grabbed an inch of skin near Zack's elbow and gave it a twist.

"Ow!" Zack yelped with a grin. "All right already! I believe it!"

The door to the bus popped open and a guy with a silver whistle and a clipboard ducked his head out. As soon as he saw us, a slow, easy smile spread across his face like warm butter on hot toast.

"Hey, gang!" he shouted. "Where we goin' today?"

"CAMP BEE-A-CHAMP!" we hollered. There were only five of us from our side of town—me, Zack, Walker, Sam Sherman, and Tony Anzaldi. You'd never have guessed from listening to us yell though. We sounded like the crowd at the final game of the NCAA championships.

"All RI-I-I-I-I-GHT!" the guy on the steps shouted. "That's the spirit! My name's Scott, and I'm going to be one of your counselors this week."

The word counselor sent a shiver of excitement down my back. Not only were we going to basketball camp—we were going to sleep-over camp. Up until that second, the farthest I'd ever been away from home overnight without my family was Zack's house. And that's just down the block.

"When I call your name, I want you to grab your gear and climb on board," Scott told us. "Sam Sherman! Where's Sam?"

The tallest kid in the pack waved a long arm. "Right here!" he called. He grabbed a black suitcase on wheels and said goodbye to his mom who was talking on a cell phone. She patted him, waved her fingers, and kept talking.

"Mickey McGhee!" Scott shouted as Sam climbed the steps to the bus.

Meggie hugged my knees so hard she almost knocked me over. Mom smoothed down the stick-up hair on top of my head and planted two kisses on my face.

"Now remember to change your underwear every day," she reminded me. At least sixteen times louder than she had to.

"Awww, Mom." I grabbed my duffel bag, tossed it onto the pile of luggage, bounded up the steps of the bus, and snagged myself a window seat. If I don't get enough air on a bus, I throw up. Or at least I think I could throw up. The only bus I've ever ridden on is the school bus, so I don't really know for sure. There was just no sense taking chances on a trip as cool as this one.

When everybody was on board, Scott waved to

the families and swung into a front seat. The doors closed behind him with a whoosh that made my heart do another jump shot.

"We're on our way, Mick!" Zack shouted, pounding my knee with his fist.

I looked out the window. Mom and Meggie waved like I was going off to fight a war instead of just to learn how to land a decent lay-up. I grinned and waved back, then looked away fast.

"Knock it off," I told Zack. "You think my knee's a punching bag, or what?"

The bus made three stops before we got out on the highway. Each time, a new bunch of guys pushed and shoved their way down the aisle. I knew a lot of them from rec department games. Our team, the Pinecrest Flying Eagles, had beaten them all to win the championship this spring.

As soon as we were out on the open road, I opened the window and let the wind roar through my hair. I still couldn't believe I was going. For somebody like me who wants to be an NBA star someday, basketball camp is like school—you just gotta go there.

"The first thing we have to do is learn the Camp Bee-a-Champ Theme Song," Scott announced. He stood in the aisle bracing himself on the seats on both sides. "Okay, here's how it goes. 'Be a champ! Be a champ! Be a cha-a-a-a-a-a-mp!' Come on everybody, try it!"

"Be a champ! Be a champ! Be a cha-a-a-a-a-a—amp!" we sang.

"Be a tramp! Be a tramp! Be a tra-a-a-a-a-a-a-amp!" Sam Sherman sang behind me. If there were A Wise Guy Award, Sam Sherman would win it—gold-plated.

By the time we got to camp, the theme song was stuck to my brain like bubble gum on the sole of a sneaker. So was *On Top Of Spaghetti*. And something about there not being any bananas in the sky, just a sun and a moon and coconut cream pie.

"Wow! Awesome!" Zack cried as we clambered down onto the gravel parking lot. "Look at that lake!"

Normally the sight of cold water rippling in the bright sun would make me want to take a flying leap and jump in. But right then I was too busy staring at the small brown cabins nestled in the pine trees to think about swimming. What if Zack and I got assigned to different cabins? What if Sam Sherman was the only person I knew in my cabin? Or worse yet—what if I didn't know anybody in my cabin?

"Okay guys! Listen up!" Scott hollered. He

blew three sharp blasts on his whistle and waved his arms in the time-out signal. "I'm going to read cabin assignments. As soon as you hear your name, grab your gear and go claim your bunk. The cabins are all numbered with a sign in front. Just take the path and head through the trees. Okay! Cabin one …"

I held my breath and tried to ignore Zack and Walker who were shoving each other and laughing.

"Mark Johnson, Darrell Ferguson, Eddie Parenti, Zack Zeno, Walker Adams …"

My heart pounded like a monster headache.

"Mickey McGhee!"

Whew! Relief! I grabbed my duffel bag and followed Zack and Walker down the twisty dirt trail to the very end of the row of cabins. Zack ran up to the small wooden porch and pushed open the door. By then, the rest of the guys had caught up with us and shoved past Walker and me to get inside. Walker followed them in, but I hung back and looked around. After the noise of the city, it seemed like we had traveled a million miles into the wilderness. I took a deep breath of fresh air and let it out. Camp Bee-a-Champ seemed like a weird place to learn the secrets of the big-city pros. But I was ready to play some serious ball.

"Hey, we saved you a bunk by us. What were you doing out there?" Walker asked as I came through the wooden screen door. It banged behind me with a sound that made me think of hot days and cold lemonade on my Grandma McGhee's screened-in porch. The thought made me wince, like I'd burned myself with the iron trying to the flatten the hem of my tee-shirt. Grandma McGhee was the one thing I didn't want to think about. She was sick. Really sick. And I was afraid she was going to die.

I blinked in the dim light and sneezed as specks of dust flew past me in a shaft of light from one of the three small windows. The cabin was one big room with plain wooden walls, a plain wooden floor, and a plain wooden ceiling. It felt like being inside a big brown box. I walked across the room to where two sets of iron bunk beds met each other in the corner.

"I got dibs on the top bunk." Walker pointed to the bed against the back of the cabin.

"I'll take the bottom of this other one," Zack said. "You wanna be on top, Mick?"

"Sure!" I gave my duffel bag a toss. It hit the side wall of the cabin before landing in front of the window. It would be pretty cool to lie in bed at night and gaze at the stars through the wavy panes of glass.

Behind me the door banged, and I thought of Grandma McGhee again.

"Okay guys, ten minutes to get settled, and then I want everyone to head over to the gym," Scott called. "But first, somebody has mail already. Which one of you is Mickey?"

I was so surprised I couldn't answer. Who would be writing me a letter this soon? I hadn't even been at camp for an hour yet!

"He's over here!" Walker called.

Scott flipped me the letter. I fumbled, then caught it against my stomach with both hands. It was in a pink envelope with a huge sticker of an ice cream sundae on the flap. My name and address marched across the front in purple ink. Without even opening it, I knew who'd sent it.

"Who's it from?" Zack and Walker asked.

"Nobody," I said, shoving it under my pillow. "Come on, let's get over to the courts."

Walker gave me a weird look. The letter was from Trish Riley, a cheerleader for the Flying Eagles. Until Walker moved here from Salt Lake City earlier in the year, she'd had a crush on me the size of California. But lately it seemed like she liked Walker too. Maybe even more. Only now maybe she didn't. I didn't care either way. I'm not interested in girls. And won't be until I'm at least 27. Maybe even 30.

Walker looked at me weird again. I shrugged and headed for the door. Walker knew the letter was from Trish, and he was disappointed not to have gotten one too. Don't ask me how I knew that. I just did. Man! I hadn't even been to camp for an hour, and already I had myself a pink and purple problem!

2

Me and Grandma McGhee

"Hey guys! Everybody settle down please!" Scott hollered.

Swarms of boys buzzed around the court like honeybees. I thought there were at least 200 of them, but Walker said he'd heard Scott say there were 105. Still, that was a lot of players. All of a sudden, I felt my knees knocking. Back home I was A team material. Here I might not even make sixth man on the tournament team.

"The first thing we need to do is separate you by age. I want everybody who will be in fourth grade this year to line up by Joe." Scott ordered. A guy wearing a red baseball cap backwards waved his arms to show that he was Joe. "Fifth graders line up by me. Sixth graders will go with Mark."

"Fifth graders—that's us," Zack said, already heading over toward Scott.

I trailed behind him thinking how amazing it was not to be a fourth grader any more. Fourth graders were the babies of basketball. Fifth graders had some experience.

"Okay," Scott said, when about 40 of us had formed a scraggly knot around him. "We're going to divide up into teams of eight for a shoot-out. Each player stands at the foul line, takes a shot, and passes the ball to the guy behind him. First team to hit eight points wins."

We counted off to form teams. Zack and I let a bunch of guys get in between us so we could both be Sonic Stingers. Walker made the Battling Buzzers and Sam Sherman became a Bumble Brat. That last one cracked us up because Sam Sherman had been a brat long before he ever got to Camp Bee-a-Champ.

While the other teams headed to their baskets, the Sonic Stingers lined up. A guy I knew from home, George the Giant, was first. He'd played for the Brunswick Blue Dolphins last season. They were a pretty good team, but they'd been no match for the Eagles in the championship. Even so, George was definitely somebody you'd want on your side.

I watched him stride up to the foul line like he owned it, dribble, and aim. He made landing a sinker look as easy as ABCs. George tossed the ball to the next guy and they gave each other a high five. I winced as I heard their knuckles crack against each other. I hate knuckle-fives almost as much as I hate math. The next guy missed. He ran for the ball, muttered something under his breath, and slammed it down hard on the floor so it bounced over my head. Zack caught it and started to hand it to me.

"Whoa! Time-out!" Scott hollered. "The most important thing you need to learn is teamwork. Everybody hates to miss, but it happens—even to the pros. Take the ball back and give it to the guy behind you," Scott ordered the kid who'd bounced it over my head.

The Sonic Stingers groaned in pain. All around us we could hear coaches shouting "Two! Three!" And there we were—stuck at one lousy point until some lamebrain learned how to play fair. Zack tossed the ball out on the floor, and the kid grabbed it and handed it to me. I stepped up to the foul line and shot. A miss. Quickly, I ran out, scooped up the ball and handed it to Zack. I'd shot too fast, but I couldn't help it—I'd felt rushed. It was all the bad-sport-kid's fault. If he hadn't slowed everything down, I'd have made it. Zack dribbled, scrunched up his face, and aimed. The ball sailed through the hoop smooth as whipped cream.

"Way to go!" I shouted, high-fiving him without my knuckles.

I was so bugged. I wanted to slam a few balls myself. I knew Scott was sizing us up. Now he was going to think Zack was the better player. Which wasn't even true. Zack was good, but I was so fast and tricky the local newspaper nicknamed me "Spider" McGhee. They said it's like I have eight arms and legs. But would Scott see that? No. Because before the buzzer sounded and the Battling Buzzers won the round, I'd missed a second shot.

After the shootout, we worked on passing. I'm a ball-hogger. I know it. But that's only because I want to be a star so bad that it hurts like a toothache to have to give up control. When we finished, Scott gave Zack a candy bar for being the best passer.

"Wow. That was fun," Zack said as we walked to the dining hall for dinner.

"Yeah," I muttered. Personally, I'd had more fun cleaning my room.

Walker caught up with us. "Look what I got for being the best listener on my team," he announced, holding up a candy bar just like Zack's.

"Cool," I said. Personally, I didn't think being a good listener was worth a piece of bubble gum.

We weren't at school, for Pete's sake. We were at basketball camp. We were supposed to get physical—not sit around listening to people yak. I kicked a stone all the way down the path to the dining hall.

Inside, a line had already formed in front of the steaming metal pans of food. I grabbed a plate and tried to see what was on the menu. It looked like mystery meat. Cafeteria food. I wrinkled my nose and said, "Yuck. Gross-out food."

Zack shrugged. "Smells pretty good to me. Hey, look! There's corn on the cob."

"Cool!" Walker agreed. "Hey, you guys wanna catch lightning bugs when it gets dark?"

"Lightning bugs? For what?" I asked. I couldn't believe it. Lightning bugs were stupid.

"Just to do it," Walker said with a grin "In Utah, we never had lightning bugs. I think they're awesome. The other night I caught about 15. I put 'em in a jar and then let 'em go again."

"Sure," Zack agreed. "Maybe on the way back from the game we could do it."

I didn't even want to think about the game. Scott had divided us up into the Eastern Conference and the Western Conference. Zack and I were Eastern and Walker was Western—just like it would have been if he were back in Salt

Lake. Every night teams from both conferences would square off to play mini-games. At the end, one of them from each grade would take home the championship trophy. At the rate we were going, the Sonic Stingers would be taking home the booby prize.

I grabbed some silverware and watched as a lady in a hairnet scooped a mound of mystery meat on my plate. I wondered what Mom was making for dinner back home. Probably taco salad. With ice cream for dessert. Tears stung the back of my eyes. I blinked hard and grabbed my plate. I grabbed it so fast that my ear of corn almost spun down the middle of the dining hall like a rolling pin.

"Let's sit over there by the wall." Zack pointed to an empty table. We eased through the crowd and grabbed three seats—two for us and one for Walker.

"Man, this is so fun!" Walker cried as he climbed over the bench of the picnic table and sat down. "At first I was afraid maybe I wouldn't be any good. But I'm doing okay. How about you, Mick?"

I shoved a forkful of mystery meat in my mouth and pointed wildly to show him I couldn't talk with my mouth full. By the time I swallowed he'd already changed the subject. "When you going to read your letter?" he asked me. "Who do suppose it's from? Man, that's amazing to get a letter this soon. My mom said there will probably only be time to send one, maybe two."

I shrugged. "We're only going to be here a week. Mail's no big deal."

It was a lie. Mail was a very big deal. Right then, I'd have been happy with a letter trying to get me to give money to a cat shelter. I thought about the pink and purple letter under my pillow. Suddenly, I wanted to read it more than I wanted the peach cobbler we were having for dessert.

"I'm going back to the cabin," I said, jumping up. "I've got a bad headache. If I'm gonna go to the games tonight, I better lie down."

It wasn't a lie—exactly. I didn't really have a headache, but it was true about the need to lie down and be quiet. If I didn't do it, I'd explode right through the roof of the dining hall. Before anybody could offer to come with me, I told Scott I was going back to the cabin. He gave me a look like he didn't quite believe the headache story. But he said okay, as long as I made it back for the first game. I promised I would. I didn't care. The Sonic Stingers weren't playing anyhow.

Walking along the green path to the cabin, I

thought about how excited I'd been to go to camp. How much I thought I'd learn and how much fun I'd have. But I wasn't having any fun at all. Camp was terrible. Camp was so bad it made school seem like Christmas morning. I looked up into the tops of the trees at the patches of sky glowing pink and orange and streaked with blue. Grandma McGhee always called the color of sunset sky-blue pink.

Inside, the cabin smelled musty like damp clothes and dirty socks. I climbed up on my bunk and reached under the flat pillow for my letter. Before I tore it open, I stared at the swoopy letters and the tiny heart dotting the "i" in Mickey.

Postage 35¢

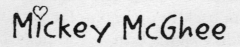

Mickey McGhee

Dear Mickey,

I'm writing this on Friday. You are still down the street. I can see you out the window acting goofy with Zack. If your mom sees you jumping your bike like that she's going to be mad. I don't blame her either.

When you get this you will be at camp. Do you like it? Don't get sunburn and watch out for ticks. You can get Lime Disease if one bites you. Stop! Don't say it! I can already hear you saying that Lime Disease is better than Lemon Disease. It's not funny Mickey McGhee. Also watch for miskeetoes. I think they have a disease too, but I forget what it is.

I am going to cheerleading camp next month. Since I wrote to you, you have to write to me, OK?

Have you learned any good ghost stories? Did anything scary happen? Remember to tell me.

I have to go. I hear the ice cream truck outside. I miss you. Well, I don't yet because you're still outside screaming. You are so loud you should get arrested for disturbing the peace. But I WILL miss you. I know it.

From,

Trish.

Carefully, I folded up the letter and put it back in the envelope. It seemed like a lifetime ago that I'd jumped my bike and run around the neighborhood hollering. It had only been three days. Since then, the world had done a somersault. Grandma McGhee had gone to the hospital in the middle of the night in an ambulance. And I'd gone far away to a goofy camp where everything was named after bees.

I closed my eyes and said a prayer. *God, please bless Grandma McGhee—and me.*

3

Red Eyes and Fireflies

"Wow! That sure was a cliff-hanger!" Zack exclaimed as we walked back to our cabin after the game. A team called the Clover Crunchers had swatted The Swarm out of the contest in the last two minutes of play. Tomorrow night my team, the Sonic Stingers, would battle a team called the Pollenators.

Walker darted ahead of us and grabbed at the air. "Whoa! Check this!" he shouted. He ran back to show us two fireflies tickling the cup of his hand. "I caught 'em both at once."

Lightning bugs were so thick on the path it was like walking into a shower of twinkling Christmas lights. "Wow. There sure are a lot of them here," I admitted. "We don't get near this many at home."

"That's because they're dying out in the city," Zack said. "Too many chemicals." He grabbed a bug, then let it go almost right away. "You know what some people do to lightning bugs?" he asked Walker. "They try to yank their lights out while they're still lit. Then they stick 'em on themselves so they glow in the dark."

"That's disgusting," I snapped. "And mean too." I jammed my hands in my pockets and walked faster. No bug deserved to be treated like that. Not even a tarantula. Suddenly I remembered something Grandma McGhee told me one time, about a trip she'd taken with my grandpa when they were young. "I know something really cool about fireflies, though," I said, slowing down again.

"What's that?" Walker asked, watching the two he'd caught travel up his arm on their skinny, little bug legs.

I tried to remember where exactly she'd said this happened, but the name of the state refused to come out from its hiding place in my brain. "There's a town in the Great Smoky Mountains where all the fireflies light up at the same time."

"No way!" Zack cried. "You're making that up." He punched my arm and laughed. "That's a good one though."

"I am NOT making it up," I argued. "My grandmother saw them one time. She said it's like a wave of light coming at you so bright you can actually see where you're going in the pitch dark.

She said fireflies give off pure light because none of it's wasted on heat."

"I'd sure like to see them all lighting up at once," Walker said as one of his two bugs took flight.

So would I, I thought. *I'd like to be on a family vacation in the Great Smoky Mountains with my grandma watching for the firefly light right this minute.* But that would never happen. She was lying in a hospital with scary tubes sticking out of her. And I was here. Anyway, our family vacation is always the same. We spend two days at Cedar Point, an amusement park in Sandusky, Ohio. And stay in a motel with a pool. Up ahead, I could hear guys screaming as they tried to scare each other in the dark.

"Did you SEE that?" Walker yelped. "A bat swooped so low I thought it was going to buzz the top of my head."

He and Zack started arguing about whether or not bats can really get caught in people's hair. I tuned them out. All I wanted to do was go back to the bunk and try and catch some sleep.

At the cabin I ran ahead, up the porch steps, and inside, careful not to bang the screen door.

"Hey, we're going to have a junk food feast!" one of the guys named Eddie called when I came in. "Scott says we can have a snack before lights out."

The thought of nacho-flavored Doritos perked me up. I'd been kind of bummed when the counselors had collected all our snacks from home. They'd stashed them in a big plastic tub under Scott's bed in the counselor's cabin. They said it was so wild animals didn't get it. But we all knew they just didn't want us pigging out.

The door opened behind me, and Zack and Walker came in with Scott who was carrying the blue tub of goodies. As soon as the lid came off, guys fell on that stuff like they'd hiked the Oregon Trail with nothing to eat but a few nuts and berries. I grabbed my Doritos and started to climb up on my bunk.

"Wait a minute guys!" Scott called. "Before you get too comfortable, I've got a sign up sheet here." He waved the clipboard Walker said must be attached to his hand with Super-Glue. "Everybody needs to sign up for a chore."

A huge groan filled the cabin. "Chores? What kind of chores?" the guy named Eddie demanded. "I thought this was supposed to be fun!"

"It is," Scott said. "But there's stuff that's got to be done. Whoever signs up first gets to pick the best jobs. If you don't sign up, you'll get the dreaded ..." he rolled his eyes and made a face, "... outhouse duty!"

"Ewwwwwwwwwww!" We all held our noses and pretend-gagged. For a second, I forgot I was feeling bad.

I ran over, grabbed the pen, and signed myself up for breakfast duty the next morning. Walker signed up for the same thing.

"You guys are nuts," Zack told us, taking a bite out of a Twinkie. "You just signed yourselves up for getting up at six o'clock in the morning. Everybody else will get an extra hour of sleep."

Walker and I looked at each other and shrugged. Getting up early beat outhouse duty any day. At 10:30 P.M., Scott flickered the lights in the cabin and told us it was time to "hit the hay." I crawled under the thin sheet in the dark and stared at the black square of window. The quarter moon peaked between the pine trees like a shiny, white, capital C. It was hard to believe that moon was the same moon that was shining over my house on Arvin Avenue at the very same minute. I was so tired. Only I couldn't sleep. I lay there in the dark, listening to the scurry of animal feet through the leaves.

"Miiiiiiiiiii-keeeeeeeeee. Miiiiiiiiiii-keeeee!"

A deep, whispery voice broke the silence.

Thumpety-bump! My heart did two beats at once. I grabbed the sheet under my chin and held still, every muscle tensed

"Miiiiiiii-keeeeeee!

It was hoarser this time. I sat up with a jerk and looked around. The only sound inside the cabin was the little whistle Zack's nose always makes when he sleeps.

"I can seeeeeeeeeeeee you!"

Goosebumps popped out on my arms like chicken pox.

"I can seeeeeeeee you, Mickeeeeeeeeee!"

"Zack?" I croaked in a loud whisper. "Zack?"

No answer.

"Walker?"

No answer.

I crawled to my knees and groped for my flashlight. Scott had told us to take our flashlights to bed in case we needed to get up in the middle of the night. I found mine by my feet and aimed it toward the window. My fingers fumbled with the switch. Two red eyes stared back at me through the glass.

Before I could stop myself, I screamed. The flashlight fell out of my hand and rolled off the bunk.

"What's wrong? WHAT?" Zack hollered

below me. His feet hit the bare wood floor with a thud.

Next to me, I could hear Walker sitting up. "Mickey? What happened?" he asked in a groggy voice.

Everywhere guys were screaming, jumping out of bed, and groping for flashlights.

Suddenly, the front door opened with a bang.

"WHAT'S GOING ON IN HERE?" Scott shouted, flooding the room with light. His hair stuck out of his head in 50 directions and he was barefoot. He was wearing a Miami University T-shirt and plaid boxer shorts.

"We don't know!" Darrell Ferguson croaked. "Somebody screamed."

Scott let out a sigh and ran his hands through his wild hair. "Okay, who screamed?" he demanded.

I sat in the middle of my bunk feeling like a total jerk. "I did," I said no louder than I had to.

Scott came over to my bunk. "What did you do that for? You have a nightmare?"

I shook my head no. "There was something outside the window. I—I heard it and when I looked there were ..." Everybody was staring at me. I took a deep breath and blurted out the rest. "There were two red eyes looking in at me."

Scott's laugh surprised me so much I blinked. "Oh, you city kids!" he scoffed. "Every year one of you gets spooked. Those red eyes belonged to a raccoon. They're all over out here. Look." He flipped off the overhead light and plunged the cabin into darkness again. Then he shone his flashlight at the window. Sure enough, two fat raccoons looked over at us like we were interrupting their dinner. Which, of course, we were. One sat under the bird feeder, and the other had climbed up the pole and was sitting on the tray. Both of them gobbled birdseed like they'd sprouted wings.

"See?" Scott said. "Nothing to be afraid of. Now everybody go back to sleep. Mickey, you and Walker have to rise and shine at six. It's time to cop some serious 'Zs.'"

When Scott was gone, I lay back down and thought about the raccoons. There was no question that one of them had been staring at me in the dark. But that still didn't account for one very important thing I hadn't said. Unless they were Hollywood raccoons, it wasn't likely any of them were outside calling me by name. I lay still as stone listening for the terrible voice again. But all I heard was an owl hooting in the distance.

No Joke!

Six o'clock came early. I sat up, rubbed my eyes, and looked at Walker. He looked like a zombie staring straight ahead with his mouth hanging open like he was catching flies. Somehow he got down off the bunk, onto the floor, and into some clothes. But he didn't look normal until we came back from the outhouse and headed for the dining hall.

"It's neat being the only ones up, isn't it?" he asked as we walked along the edge of the water. We'd cheated and taken the long way around the lake to do our breakfast chores.

"Yeah," I agreed. The morning hush and the new sun rising made me feel like God was walking along with us. I figured He was getting as big a kick as we were out of the scaredy-cat frogs plopping into the water.

"What happened to you last night, Mick?" Walker asked after a giant croaker make a noisy splash. "Did you really get scared of a raccoon?

33

We've got raccoons back home."

I shrugged and thought about whether or not to tell him what I'd heard. Now that it was light outside it seemed pretty stupid. But I really had heard it—and it had been as scary as something out of a horror movie. "Did you—uh—hear anything last night?" I asked him. "Besides the raccoons I mean."

"Nope. Like what?" Walker picked up a stone and sent it skimming across the surface of the lake.

I watched the ripples make rings in the water and decided not to tell after all. "Nothing. I must have been dreaming or something," I answered. "Come on—we better hurry."

Sam Sherman greeted us as soon as we walked in the back door of the kitchen. He stood at a counter in the center of the room filling glasses of milk and juice from two big, plastic jugs. "It's about time you got here," he said. I took that to mean good morning.

A thought skittered across my mind on little raccoon feet. Would Sam have snuck out of his cabin somehow and called my name last night? Ever since kindergarten, Sam had made it his job to make my life miserable. Lately we'd sort of called a truce, but this was the kind of thing he'd think was funnier than the Sunday comics. I eyed him warily and didn't say anything.

"Here—give me that tray of milk. I'll take it out front," Walker said to him.

"NO!" Sam snapped. "I mean, no, I can do it. You guys can fill the silverware baskets."

Walker and I looked at each other and rolled our eyes. If Sam thought there was something special about carrying trays that weigh a ton, let him carry them. We worked fast and finished up our chores just as the first bunch of guys burst through the door. The smell of fried bacon had their tongues hanging out.

"I'll save you guys the same seats we had last night," Zack told me and Walker as he grabbed a tray and got in line.

"That's okay," the kitchen lady with the hairnet told us. "You boys go ahead and get yourselves some food. You did a good job."

Walker and I got in line behind Zack. Breakfast looked as good to me as last night's dinner had looked disgusting. *Maybe I was starting to get into the swing of this camp thing,* I thought. I set my loaded tray on the table and climbed over the bench. Scrambled eggs, bacon, and pancakes with plenty of butter and syrup sure beat mystery meat. I grabbed my milk and took a big gulp.

"EWWW" Milk spit out of my mouth and

splashed all over my breakfast. I tried to jump up, but couldn't get my legs over the bench fast enough. "OH GROSS! GROOOOOOOOOSS!"

A zillion pairs of eyes looked at me, but I was too shocked to care. The milk was spoiled! And not just sour either. Soft white curdles had banged into my teeth and slid down my throat. I was probably poisoned!

Scott got out of the food line and rushed over. "What's the matter, Mickey?" he asked. He didn't say "now," but you could hear it in his voice.

"My milk's spoiled." I grabbed my T-shirt and started scrubbing my tongue.

"That's weird. Mine's not," Zack said.

Scott tried to hide a sigh, but it escaped anyhow. He picked up my glass and took a sniff. "Smell's fine to me," he announced.

He started to set it back on the table, then brought it back to his face. He didn't smell it again, but he looked inside. Hard. Every eye in the room watched as he walked over to the food line and came back with an empty coffee cup. Slowly, he poured the milk from my glass into the empty cup. White chunks of curdled milk fell like pieces of ice from a glass of soda. All around me guys shoved aside their glasses. Their faces were as white as the curdled milk.

Scott burst out laughing. "Just as I thought," he said. "Oldest trick in the book. They're marshmallows, Mickey. Plain old mini-marshmallows."

I could feel my face turning redder than a cardinal on a snowbank. I glared at Sam Sherman. He returned the look with a laugh. No wonder he hadn't wanted me or Walker to take out the trays of milk and juice. He'd wanted to be sure I got the glass with the marshmallows. That did it! Now I knew the score. Sam Sherman was up to his old tricks again. It had been him last night outside my window. For sure.

By the time we finished eating, Sam had already left the dining hall. I wanted to tell him I knew he'd snuck out of his cabin and tried to scare me. But I decided to tell Zack and Walker first.

"Wow," Zack said when I finished the story. "No wonder you screamed. That Sam! Marshmallows in milk are one thing, but scaring people at night is something else. You going to tell Scott?"

I shook my head no. Scott thought I was a wuss. I could tell. And who could blame him? I had to prove myself on the basketball court before I said anything about scary voices in the middle of the night. But as soon as we turned up at the gym, I could see that it was going to be a bad morning.

The coaches were still stuck on passing. It's like they had passing on the brain. Scott lined us up in three columns at the half court mark.

"The guy in the middle column gets the ball," Scott explained. "His job is to lock eyes with me and keep them locked. No glances to the right or left. No cheating. I'm talking serious eye-lock here. The player with the ball starts the fast break, and the wings—those are the two guys on either side—break to the goal. It's the ball handler's job to make a pass to one of the wings. But remember—eyes on me the entire time. Got that?"

"Yeah, but what do the wings learn?" Sam Sherman demanded. He was in the right column and I was in the middle. "That seems like a waste of time for us."

I couldn't believe that guy! Only Sam would question the coaches. If he were back at Pinecrest Park and asked Coach Duffy a question like that, he'd be running laps or doing push-ups by now.

Scott seemed happy enough to explain. "Good question," he said. "It does seem like the wings have it easy. But the fact is, your job is to drive the gaps and position yourself in the ball handler's line of vision. Don't forget—he who has the ball scores the points."

"Oh yeah." Sam looked embarrassed. A fact

that made me happier than it probably should have.

When my turn came to make the break, I stared at Scott's brown eyes and ran forward. But then, before I could stop myself, I looked to my right. Just one tiny glance. Scott shrilled his whistle.

"No good!" he hollered. "You can't look away Mickey, not even for a second. You do that and you set the other team up to cop a steal."

I knew that! But it was like my eyes had a mind of their own. We tried it again, and the second time I did better. But my heart wasn't in it anymore. I didn't understand what was happening. Somehow I'd gone from being a star to being the biggest dud on the court. Scott probably thought I should take up soccer. Or, worse yet, learn how to play chess. By the time he blew his whistle at 11:15 A.M. to announce that we could go swimming before lunch, I thought he might be right.

"What's wrong, Mick?" Zack asked as we headed back to the cabin. "You don't seem like you're having much fun. Don't you like camp?"

I walked fast. We had to change into swim shorts and be back at the lake in 15 minutes flat. No one could stick a toe in the water until everyone was there and counted. "I'm having fun," I protested. I knew I didn't sound too convincing.

"Is that Sam thing bugging you?" Zack asked.

"Yeah. No. I don't know." There was a bunch of stuff bugging me—Sam and his tricks, my grandma being sick, and the fact that I was making such a bad showing on the court. Who knew which one bugged me most?

"Well, if it's Sam, forget about him. He's just being Sam. You know how he is. I didn't think he bothered you so much any more."

I shrugged. I knew Zack was trying to help, but I didn't want to talk about it. I picked up my pace, glad to see the cabin in sight up ahead. "Come on," I said to Zack and Walker. "Let's get changed. Last one ready's a rotten egg!"

We ran inside, made like quick-change artists, and high-tailed it back to the lake before anyone else did. Scott was already there talking with a lady lifeguard. When she heard us bursting down the path she climbed up into her high white chair with a pair of binoculars.

The second every nose was counted we jumped in the water. It felt so good I forgot about everything but the sun and the pleasure of splashing around. I lay on my back and floated for awhile before Walker came up alongside me.

"Hey, wanna go in the boat?" he asked. "Scott

says we can take the canoe out if we wear life jackets."

"Yeah!" I flipped over and made my way to shore. I'd never paddled a real canoe before.

Scott handed out orange safety vests, and Walker, Zack, and I each put one on. We were already in the canoe before I saw who was going to take the seat in front. I almost stood up and got out, but I didn't want to make another scene. At least I was in the back. Scott pushed us offshore and we glided out with Sam Sherman paddling in front and Zack in the very back. Sam kept shouting instructions to Zack like Zack was too dumb to figure out how to do it. But finally he quieted down, and we drifted around the sun-dappled lake. It made me think of pioneers back in the early days of America.

"Hey, Mickey!" Sam hollered suddenly. My pioneer daydream ended with a jolt. "What's that cheer the cheerleaders do? You know the one. 'Lean to the left, lean to the right, stand up ...'"

Water closed in over my head. I sputtered and grabbed hold of the side of the canoe.

When Sam came up from under the water, he finished his cheer, "Splash down! Fight! Fight! Fight!"

It was supposed to be "Stand up, sit down!

Fight! Fight! Fight!" But I wasn't about to say so. I crawled back into the canoe after Walker and Zack, dripping like wet laundry. If standing up in the canoe was Sam's idea of a joke, it was fine with me. At least I was dressed for it.

Thumps in the Night

"Go Mickey! Go Mickey! Go Mickey!" Walker chanted from the stands. I kept trying to go, but my go was gone.

One minute left on the clock and I'd scored a lousy two points. The handwriting was all over the court. The game belonged to two people—and neither of them was me. Sam Sherman led the Bumble Brats and George the Giant ruled the Sonic Stingers.

"Go Mickey! Go Mickey! Go Mickey!"

Walker's voice pushed me forward. Twenty seconds left. I grabbed a steal and made a run to the basket. Zip! In between two Bumble Brats. Zap! Around a third.

STOP!

Sam Sherman leaped in front of me. Did I dare shoot over his head? No way! I kept my eyes on Sam and passed. Zack grabbed the ball and broke to the paint. One toss and in it sailed, sweet as sugar.

We won!

I walked off the court and slumped down next to Walker.

"That was sooooooooo cool!" Walker shouted. "Zack really nailed that last shot. I hope my team does that well."

I shrugged. Who cared about the Sonic Stingers anyway? My real team was the Pinecrest Flying Eagles. In a week, all of this would be over and nobody would even remember who'd taken home the trophy. These fake teams were so bogus they weren't even worth thinking about.

"Come on, let's get back to the cabin," I said, getting to my feet. "Maybe Scott will let us have a snack again. We're going ahead, Zack!" I hollered over my shoulder.

Zack didn't answer. He was too busy pounding a bunch of guys on the back and letting them pound him. I sighed and pushed open the door.

"Mickey! Hey! Wait up!" Scott called.

I didn't want to wait up. And I especially didn't want to talk to Scott. I could see inside his brain as clear as if I had an x-ray camera. He was thinking what a loser I was. I waited by the door, ready to make my escape.

"I just wanted to tell you what a great job you did there at that final shot," he said. He came over and ruffled my hair.

"Huh?" I stared at him. Was he kidding? He had to be. I'd tried to make a break for the basket and it hadn't worked.

"Yeah, you did that pass exactly like I showed you. Exactly! Good job! I know how hard it is to give up the ball. Whew! I remember my team-mates practically had to pry it out of my hands when I was your age."

"They did?" Scott was a big time player at Miami University in Oxford, Ohio. I couldn't believe he `adn't been born a team player. Teamwork was all he ever talked about.

"You bet! Anyway, I just wanted to tell you I noticed. You made a real difference tonight." He clapped me on the shoulder and went out the door.

All the way back to the cabin, Walker jabbered about his Uncle Dwight who was an artist in San Francisco. He was coming to visit as soon as camp was over. I only half-listened. My brain was flashing something so huge it's a wonder I wasn't glowing in the dark.

"Wow!" I said out loud.

"Wow, what?" Walker asked. He grabbed for a lightning bug and missed.

"I just realized something about passing."

"Cool!" He darted in front of me and grabbed at a bug.

He wasn't paying attention. I was too dazzled by my own thoughts to care. I'd always thought passing was sissy. I'd thought it meant you didn't have the right stuff to make the dunk yourself. But that wasn't true. Passing meant helping your teammate. And trusting him. And getting out of the way so he could do what he needed to do to help you. Passing the ball was just like passing my problems to God! I handed 'em over, trusted Him to take care of them, and then got out of His way. I was so tickled to have thought of that I started whistling. If you happen to like Yankee Doodle, I'm actually a pretty good whistler.

Back at the cabin I ate a chocolate chip granola bar. When Scott hollered "Lights out," I crawled into bed, said my prayers, and fell asleep. Right away I started having a cool dream about a car shaped like a basketball shoe. It had glow-in-the-dark wheels and was like a dodge-'em car at an amusement park. Crash! I bashed it into Sam Sherman's car that was shaped like a hot dog in a bun. Boom! He crashed the hot dog car into mine. I steered hard to the right ...

My eyes snapped open.

Thump.

Thump.

Thump.

I sat up in bed and looked around. The sound stopped. I held my breath and waited. It started again, louder this time. The hairs on the back of my neck stood up. It was coming from right outside the window! Carefully, I crawled over to it and shined my flashlight. Goosebumps raced up my arms. Nothing. Nobody was there. But the sound kept going.

Thump.

Thump.

Thump.

Sam Sherman. It had to be. But how was he doing it? Carefully, I slipped down off the bunk. My feet hit the floor with a muffled thud that made Zack mutter something and roll over. Slowly, I made my way outside. The inside door stood open to let the breeze blow through the screen. I pushed the screen door gently, walked out, and closed it silently behind me.

Everywhere I looked, blackness wrapped itself around the campgrounds. Night in the city is dark. But night in the wilderness grabs you by the throat and shakes you like a tree in a thunderstorm. Even your insides shiver. Now that I was actually out in the darkness, it didn't seem like such a good idea anymore. Especially since I had to walk all the way around to the back of the cabin to see what was going on. Maybe I'd just walk to the corner of the building, I decided. I could sneak a peak from there. If anyone was hiding, sooner or later they'd run one way or the other.

I edged up to the side of the building and inched my way along the porch rail. When I ran out of long rail, I turned and followed the short piece around to the side. Then I felt for the rough wood of the cabin itself and moved along that. Stones dug into the soles of my bare feet. I stumbled on a root and tried not to think about what else I might step on. At the corner, I stopped. The sound was not as loud, but I could still hear it—a steady, dull ...

Thump.

Thump.

Thump.

I shined my flashlight low to the ground, praying nobody in the cabins would wake up and see it.

The sound continued. Then stopped.

Every muscle in my body tensed. Nothing happened. Nobody ran. No bushes moved. Not even a shadow flitted by in the darkness. I waited. Still nothing. The only sound was a light breeze shimmering through the pines. One last time I ran my flashlight low to the ground, but there was no one there. Slowly, I made my way back to the cabin the same way I'd come.

Inside, I tiptoed across the big room to my bunk. I had to feel around with my foot before I found a good place to get a leg up. Parts of Zack hung off of the edge of the mattress. I wedged my foot in next to his chest, and hoisted myself up. A hand closed around my foot.

"Shhhhhhhhhh!" Zack whispered. "Don't yell. It's just me."

I choked back a yelp and dropped back to the floor as he let go of my foot. "What'd you do that for?" I demanded. "Man, Zack! You scared me!"

"What were you doing outside?" he whispered again. He sat up and patted his mattress for me to sit down beside him.

I sank down and ran my fingers through my hair. Suddenly I felt too tired to talk.

"Did you hear it again?" Zack pressed. "Did you hear the voice?"

I shook my head no.

"Then what were you outside for?"

"Nothing. I'm going to bed." I didn't want to say what I'd heard. Nobody would believe it. I barely believed it myself even though I knew deep in my bones what had made the horrible thumping.

"Come on!" Zack whispered, louder. "You can tell me. I won't say a word to anybody. I promise!"

I sat on the edge of the bunk and thought about it. Zack was my best friend. We'd shared a lot of stuff. But Zack wasn't like me. He didn't imagine things that weren't there like I did. He never got spooked—or at least not as often as I did. Mom said it was because I had a vivid imagination and Zack was more practical. Maybe so. But I knew what I'd heard and I also knew what had made the noises.

"Come on!" Zack begged. "Tell me! Please?"

I sighed. "Okay. But if you laugh, I'm going to sign you up for outhouse duty. I mean it!"

"I won't laugh," Zack promised. "Honest."

"All right then." I leaned in toward him and lowered my voice to barely a murmur. "I heard— a heart."

"A heart?" Zack's eyes bugged out.

"Yes, a heart," I repeated. "A beating heart."

Another Pink and
Purple Problem

"Mail call!" Scott shouted from the doorway. "Lot of stuff today, boys!"

Guys rushed forward as though Scott were a rock star handing out signed photos. Every hand waved in the air except mine. I wanted mail. But then again I didn't. The pink and purple letter still stood between me and Walker like a brick wall. He hadn't brought it up lately, but I knew his feelings were hurt. Zack got a letter from his dad and Jo. Walker got one from his mom and one from his sister, Lindsey, plus a funny postcard from his Aunt Nancy.

"Mickey—two for you today," Scott said. He reached over some heads and handed me my letters. The one on top came in a pink envelope with purple writing marching across the front for everybody to see. I flipped it over. A big green frog sticker grinned at me.

"You got another letter from that same person," Walker said right away.

I shrugged. "I also got a letter from my mom and dad."

I turned away and went to my bunk to tear open the letter from my parents. I wanted to hear what was happening back home. I missed everybody so much it made my heart hurt. But I was afraid to hear what they would say about Grandma McGhee. My eyes scanned the first side of the page, then the second. My dog Muggsy missed me so bad he'd chewed up my Cleveland Cavs T-shirt and had started carrying the sleeves everywhere he went. That part made me laugh. Meggie missed me too. She and Dulcie, the little girl across the street, were working on a chalk design on the basketball court in the driveway to welcome me home. They hoped it wouldn't rain. That made me smile too.

The next part turned the grin upside-down. Grandma McGhee was still in the hospital. She couldn't talk, and she could only move one foot. The doctor said she'd had a stroke. I didn't know what a stroke was, but I knew it was bad. Really bad. Tears flooded my eyes. I squeezed them shut and asked God to take care of her. Then I picked up the pink envelope and carefully opened it.

Dear Mickey,

Are you having fun yet? I'm not. I have a rash on my leg. I think it's poison ivy. You could get that too if you aren't careful. Be careful. It itches.

Did you have a campfire? Camps are scary. I think ghosts live there. At least that's what I heard. I can't wait to hear all about it. Be sure to remember the good parts.

Yesterday me and Brittany went to the mall. I got blue nail polish with sparkles. I will wear it when I see you. I think it makes me look like a mermaid.

I miss you.

Trish.

I shook my head at the mermaid part. Who ever heard of a mermaid with braces on her teeth?

"Hey, guess what?" Zack called from his bunk below mine. "Jo and my dad are buying a new car. I get to help pick it out when I get back. And Jo says she will help me paint my room. What color do you think I should get?"

I didn't care about paint. But I knew it was important to Zack. His dad getting married had been a real shock to him. His real mom left when he was a baby, and he figured he and his dad didn't need another one. But Jo was cool, and Zack was starting to like her a little. I could tell.

"Blue. Get blue," I called back.

"Blue? I was thinking green. And maybe a wallpaper border with basketballs on it or something."

I couldn't help it. A huge laugh snorted through my nose. "Do you HEAR yourself?" I sputtered, hanging my head over the side of the bunk to get a look at him. "You sound like a decorating person on that TV channel all the moms like on cable." We didn't have cable TV at our house, but I knew about the channel because it was always on at Walker's and Sam's houses.

Zack laughed. "Alright already! Forget it! Hey, have you talked to Sam yet? We have free period for another half-hour. Want to go find him? I'll go with you."

I stuffed my mail under my pillow and jumped down off my bed. "Yeah, good idea."

"What's a good idea?" Walker asked from his bunk. "You guys goin' somewhere? Can I come too?"

Zack and I exchanged glances. Walker didn't know about the beating heart, and I still hadn't decided whether or not to tell him. Zack shrugged to let me know it was up to me.

"Okay," I agreed, "but come outside first. We have to tell you something, and if you dare laugh ..."

"He'll sign you up for outhouse duty!" Zack snickered.

"I won't laugh," Walker said. "Promise."

We went outside behind the cabin, and I told the story of the beating heart. "I'm sure it was Sam. But how do you suppose he did it?" I asked when I was finished. "I saw absolutely no one. I mean it. No one."

Walker shook his head. "I don't know. You sure it was a beating heart? That sounds pretty weird."

I nodded. "Yeah it was a heart all right. I know it was."

"Okay then, if you say so." He didn't laugh, but I could see a grin lurking in his eyes. He thought I was nuts. "Hey, you never did tell us who wrote you those letters in the pink envelopes," he accused.

Cornered! It was bound to have happened sooner or later. I stared at a squirrel stuffing his face at the bird feeder. There was no sense hiding the truth. He'd find out when we got home anyway. "It's no big deal," I muttered. "Just Trish Riley. She's such a goofy girl."

"I don't think so," Walker said. "I think she's nice."

"She's okay," I agreed. "But she's no big deal. Come on, we better go talk to Sam. You coming?"

Walker shook his head. "No, you guys go. I think I'm gonna walk over to the stables and look at the horses. They have two. Scott says some lady might let us pet them. We aren't allowed to ride, though."

Zack and I headed to Sam's cabin, which was just around the curve of the trail from ours. *Walker didn't come with us because he was jealous,* I told myself as I pushed branches out of our path. He felt bad that Trish hadn't written to him too. The weird part was that I would've been happy to give him my letters if it would've made him happy. He could read about blue nail polish and mermaids all he wanted.

We finally got to Sam's cabin. In front of Sam's cabin, Zack and I stood and looked at each other. "Are we supposed to knock, or what?" Zack asked.

I shrugged and went to the screen door.

Cupping my hands around my eyes, I stuck my nose flat against the screen and looked in. Sam danced by himself in the middle of the room to a noisy band on the radio.

"Check it out!" I whispered to Zack. He joined me at the door, and we looked in together. We couldn't help it—we laughed like hyenas.

Sam heard us and stopped dancing. "You guys want something?" he barked, flipping the dial on the radio to off.

"Yeah." I opened the door and Zack followed me inside. "You think you're so funny with the marshmallows and turning the canoe upside down. Those were pretty good jokes—I'll give you that. You really got me. But I'm getting a little tired of the night thing, Sam."

Sam looked at me like I'd sprouted a second head. "What night thing?"

"You know ..." All of a sudden I felt less sure of myself. "What you've been doing after lights-out."

Sam's face folded into a frown. "No, I don't know. Tell me."

"No way!" Zack said. "You already know. You just want Mickey to say it so you can make fun of him."

Sam's frown deepened. "Listen," he said, staring me straight in the eye. "I admit I'm guilty of the marshmallow trick. And you already know I tipped the canoe, but I have NOT been doing anything at night. You can ask anybody here if I've been out of the cabin." He turned to a couple guys playing a hand-held video game in the corner. One of them was my friend Tony Anzaldi from back home. "Hey guys, have I been out after dark any night?" he asked them.

"Nope," said a guy with glasses I didn't know.

"No, Mick, he hasn't," Tony agreed. "I would know because he sleeps right above me, and I'm a light sleeper."

I looked into Sam's eyes one last time and saw that he was telling the truth. Only now I had myself a real mystery. If Sam wasn't guilty of trying to scare me, who was? No way would Tony do something like that. He wasn't that kind of guy.

"Okay, then," I said. "Sorry to bother you. Come on, Zack."

"Wait!" Sam called, running after us. "You never did tell me what's happening."

"And I'm not going to," I replied. "It's not a big deal."

Another lie. It was a very big deal. Somebody was trying to scare me. Maybe they were out to get me. Or else ... I remembered what Trish had said in her letter about ghosts living at camp-grounds. But that was too silly—even for me. There weren't any ghosts. Somebody at Camp Bee-a-Champ just had a warped sense of humor.

"So now what?" Zack asked when we'd round-ed the bend to our own cabin. "I believe him, don't you?"

"Yeah, I do." I agreed. I just didn't want to believe him, because now I had nobody to blame.

No shouts or laughing greeted us when we got back to our own cabin. The whole place looked empty. I started to say that we might as well wan-der over to the horse barn and check out the hors-es. But for some reason, I opened the door and went inside ... just in time to see Walker shove two pink and purple letters back under my pillow.

7

Busted!

I opened my mouth and shut it again. I couldn't believe my eyes. Walker was my friend. What was he doing snooping around in my mail? But then I remembered that it was only Trish's letters he'd had in his hand—not the one from Mom and Dad. He must have a crush the size of Texas on that goofy girl.

"Hi," I said casually. "Thought you were going to see the horses."

Walker shrugged. "Changed my mind. It's too hot to walk all the way over there and then have to turn right around again for dinner."

Did he look guilty? I couldn't be sure. I decided to let it pass. There was nothing private in those letters anyhow. Except maybe the part about Trish wanting me to see her blue nail polish. "Yeah," I agreed. "It's hot all right." I yawned like I was either really tired or really bored.

"Did you talk to Sam?" Walker asked. He

picked up a book he'd brought from home and climbed up on his bunk with it.

"Yeah. He didn't do it though."

"Really? So who do you think did?"

A crazy thought flitted across my mind. Could Walker have done it? If he were snooping in my mail, maybe it wasn't such a reach to think he'd try to scare me too. But that was crazy. He'd been sound asleep in the bunk next to mine the whole time.

I shrugged. "No clue."

The screen door opened, then slammed shut behind me. "Hey, guys! Where is everybody?" It was Scott, frowning at his watch. "The whole cabin should be back by now. I have something to tell you all before you head over to dinner."

"What's that?" Walker asked from his bunk.

Scott grinned. "It's about the Talent Show. We always have a Talent Show every year during camp. We build a campfire in front of the dining hall and use the porch as a stage."

My heart took a nosedive. I didn't have any talent. Except for basketball. And even that was looking doubtful. "Do we have to be in it?" I asked.

"Sure," Scott answered. "It's fun. You guys can team up and do a skit if you don't have anything of your own. It's no sweat. It's just for fun. We have a ton of costumes."

"Cool!" Walker cried. He hopped down off his bunk and started playing an imaginary guitar.

"I guess I could do a skit," Zack offered. He sounded about as excited as I felt.

I didn't say anything. I didn't want to do a skit. It reminded me of doing stupid plays for school. I'm not into that stuff. I came here to play basketball not be an actor. I shoved the Talent Show out of my mind and thought about tonight's game against the Pollenators. By the time the rest of the guys came banging through the cabin door, I could feel my knees knocking. The morning's drills had all focused on passing again.

This time it had been a bounce pass drill. Talk about boring! We'd all had to stand in a circle with one guy in the middle defending. Somebody in the circle got the ball and shot to somebody else in the circle. The defender then had to try to intercept the ball. The stupid part was that he had to stay in the center of the circle even after he intercepted a pass. No fast breaks to the hoop, no 3-pointers, no shooting at all. It was mega-dumb. Besides, I figured after last night I had passing down cold. What I needed was to work on my jump shot.

"You nervous?" Zack asked as we did warm-ups to get ready for the game. People always talk about being so nervous they have butterflies in their stomachs. In my case, I think it was fireflies doing aerobics.

"Yeah, sort of. But it's really dumb. These teams are bogus," I said, stretching my leg muscles.

"They are not," Zack argued. "Anyway, if you think they're dumb, why are you so freaked?" When I didn't answer right away, he sighed and shrugged. "Maybe you're right. It probably doesn't matter all that much who wins."

For some reason that made me feel like arguing, "That's a majorly dumb attitude," I said rudely. "What's the point of playing basketball if you don't care who wins?"

Zack gave me a strange look and didn't answer. I grabbed a towel, slung it around my neck, and walked away. I was so mixed-up I didn't even know what I thought anymore.

I knew one thing, though. I was in deep trouble the minute I stepped out on the court. In the first three minutes of play, my buddy from home, Tony Anzaldi, wrote his name all over the game. I couldn't believe it! He'd been on the bench for six months after two injuries. It should have made his skills rusty. But all it had done was make him hotter than the lit end of a firecracker.

"Tone-ee! Tone-ee! Tone-ee!"

The screams from the stands spurred him on. He got another Pollinator in on the action and together they tore the place up. I tried not to think about what this meant for me when it came to try-outs for my real team, the Flying Eagles. I'd be lying though, if I didn't admit the thought tickled my brain like a feather throughout the entire game.

Suddenly the ball whizzed toward me. I snatched it and landed a nice clean lay-up.

As soon as it came through the hoop, Tony dove for the ball, grabbed it, and pounded down the court. What happened after that still has my head spinning. We caved, man! We caved! The Sonic Stingers parted like the Red Sea and let him take a path straighter than a ruler to the Pollenator basket. After that, Scott might as well have brought out the snack tub and passed out Doritos, because the Stingers were done for the night.

Five minutes later the buzzer sounded to make it official. We'd been blasted straight out of the championships. I'd played my last game at basketball camp. I slouched off the floor and out the door without saying anything to anybody.

"Hey, Mick!" Walker called after me. I ignored him and headed back to the cabin. I knew it was stupid, but I felt so bad I could have sat down on a tree stump and howled. Camp Bee-a-Champ seemed as dark and lonely as a cave.

Mom, Dad, and Meggie were 80 miles away. Grandma McGhee was in the hospital all by herself. And I was in the middle of nowhere feeling like a loser. I sniffed loudly and looked up at the sky. Night was creeping over it on quiet feet, dragging a grayness behind that matched my mood. I tried to pray for my grandma, my lonely feelings, and the bad game as separate things. But they all came together in four sad words. *I need you God.* I said them about a hundred times on the path.

In the cabin, I climbed up on my bunk and stared at the ceiling. What if Grandma McGhee died? I shoved that thought out of mind. What if I never played good basketball again? What if it was all a big fluke and now the truth was coming out? I had no talent for basketball—I'd just gotten lucky. Tears leaked out of the sides of my eyes. I brushed them away as the guys slammed through the door. Two of them, both Pollinators, were singing the dumb Camp Bee-a-Champ theme song.

When Scott brought the snacks in, I said I had a stomachache. Zack and Walker tried tempting me with strawberry Twizzlers, but I rolled over toward the window and didn't answer. It wasn't until Scott flipped off the lights that I felt like I could breathe again. I lay still for a long time thinking.

Whoooooo! Whooooooooo! Whoooooooo!

Mickkeey McGheeeeeeeeeeeeeeee!

I'd known it was coming. Maybe in a way I'd even been waiting for it. The sound was so eerie it made me shiver from my ears to my toes. Slowly, I sat up and looked over at Walker. By the thin light of the moon, I could see his head on the pillow.

Mickey McGheeeeeeeeeeeeeeeee!

"Mick! I hear it!" Zack whispered below me. "Do you recognize the voice?"

"No," I whispered back. "Do you?"

"No, but let's be quiet and listen."

For a long time, we lay in the darkness, listening to the voice moan and wail my name. And then, as always, it stopped. Silence filled the cabin for so long I started to drift off into a sort of half sleep.

"Okay, turn it off," a voice said from out of

nowhere. Or maybe said. I wasn't sure if I really heard it, or just thought I heard it. All I know for sure is that a loud squeal and a click followed. The sounds sat me bolt upright in bed.

"Zack?" I whispered. "Did you hear that?" I hung my head over my bunk and tried to see him in the dark.

He was sitting up too. "It's a tape recorder, Mick," he whispered back. "The click was when it turned off."

"I know," I agreed. "I think it's right under the window. Want to go get it?"

Zack didn't answer. I knew he didn't want to go outside in the dark. Now that I thought about it, I wasn't so sure I wanted to either. I shivered, remembering what it had felt like last night out in the woods, in the blackest part of the night. I also thought about who might be out there pushing the buttons on the recorder.

"We better wait 'til tomorrow," I whispered. "Can you wake up early?"

"Sure," Zack whispered back. "I'm a human alarm clock."

As soon as the sky changed from black to gray, Zack shook me awake. "Come on, let's go," he said. "Don't bother getting dressed."

I slipped out of bed as quiet as a shadow and

tiptoed over to the open door. The guy named Darrell jammed a pillow over his head. Zack opened the door, and I followed him out into the first thin light of morning.

"It's around back," I whispered, taking the lead. I'd forgotten to put on my shoes. My bare feet screamed in pain as I stepped on a big stone with jagged edges. "I'll bet anything it's in the weeds."

It wasn't. The black tape recorder sat perched on a mossy little knoll right under my window. Zack and I looked at it and sucked in our breath. The owner's name was taped to the front as plain as vanilla ice cream.

8

The Ghost of Camp Bee-a-Champ

"What are you guys doing for the Talent Show?" Walker asked at breakfast.

Zack looked worried. I wasn't worried at all. I figured I'd wait 'til the last minute and see what happened. I could always go up on stage with a couple guys and do something dumb. Like pretend to be a tree in the background of their skit. I'd wave around and make faces and people would think it was a riot.

"I'm gonna do my Elvis impersonation," Walker informed us. He jumped up from his chair, twanged his invisible guitar, and snarled, "I'm so looooooonely baby."

It was so funny I nearly choked on my Cheerios. "Hey, that's pretty good," I told him. "You must like that stuff."

He nodded. "Yeah, me and my sister always do shows with my cousin Natalie. We dress up and everything. My Aunt Nancy videotapes it."

A weird thought flickered across my mind.

There was one thing I could do in the Talent Show. Only nobody knew I could do it. Not even Zack. Did I have the nerve? Probably not. Besides, I didn't have any music to do it even if I wanted to. And anyway, I'd have to feel good to do a thing like that. Right now I was the most miserable kid at camp.

"I know what we could do!" Zack cried. "Mick, you and me could do a commercial. A real one maybe. Or else we could make one up. It'd be funny."

I didn't answer. I was picturing myself on the stage doing the thing nobody knew I could do. Grandma McGhee had taught me when I was little. Sometimes I still did it for her in the kitchen of her house. She always clapped like crazy. Everybody's eyes would pop from shock when they saw me. But the kids at camp might think it was stupid. Maybe it was stupid. Forget it. I couldn't do a dumb thing like that. They'd laugh me all the way back to Pinecrest Park.

"Sure," I said to Zack. "You think of a commercial and I'll do whatever you want."

Morning drills dragged. As soon as they were over, I asked Scott if Zack and I could skip swimming and go back to the cabin to practice for the Talent Show. He said okay, as long as we stayed at the cabin and didn't wander off.

"What did you do that for?" Zack whined when everyone was gone. "I thought you weren't interested in the Talent Show."

"I'm not," I said. "But I have a great idea! It's about what we found this morning behind the cabin. Buddy, it's revenge time!"

Zack's eyes sparkled. "I wondered what you were going to do about that. What do you have in mind?"

"Follow me," I said with a grin. I led the way out the door and around the back of the cabin where we'd found the tape recorder. It was still perched on its mossy knoll by the birdfeeder where we'd left it. "We're going to make a little tape of our own," I told Zack. "But we have to hurry. We'll speed it up to about the middle and tape over what was there. Then we'll rewind it. This afternoon we'll make up a ghost story and tell it to the guys in the cabin. So when they hear our tape ..." I stopped and burst out laughing.

"Yeah, but Mick," Zack said, scratching his head. "How are we going to get it turned on tonight?"

"We won't," I said, glad for once to have thought so far ahead. "The tape recorder's owner will do it for us—same as every night."

Zack frowned. "Yeah, but Mick. There's still one thing you haven't thought of. It's been a different tape every night."

Leave it to Zack to point that out. No matter how hard I try, I always get so excited I never think things all the way through. "You're right. It won't work," I said. "I guess it was a bad idea." I started back to the cabin. Everything I thought of was stupid. I couldn't do anything right.

"No, wait! It's brilliant!" Zack called after me.

The word "brilliant" spun me around.

"Sure," he said. "We'll wait 'til everybody's asleep, then go out and pop our own tape in. Simple!"

"Who's we?" I asked. Zack would never sneak out in the dark.

Zack looked sheepish. "I think I meant you," he mumbled.

I laughed. This was going to be so funny it didn't matter that Zack was a big chicken afraid of the dark. It was the perfect revenge! It took us a long time to get it right. We had to put a T-shirt over the microphone and stuff our mouths with six pieces of bubble gum each to disguise our voices. When we finished, we stashed the tape under my pillow and gave each other a high five. By the time the rest of the guys came back from swimming, we were practicing the Taco Bell commercial.

I waited until dinner to tell our ghost story to the guys in our cabin. "Hey," I said casually. "Did anybody ever hear about the Ghost of Camp Bee-a-Champ?"

Eddie Parenti put down his chicken leg. "There's no ghost here! I've been coming to this camp for three years and I've never heard of any ghost. If there was one, I'd have heard about it by now."

I hadn't planned on that. I looked at Zack and tried again, "Well, there is one," I argued. "I know guys who have heard it. I might even have heard it myself last night. I can't be sure, though. It wasn't very loud."

"What did it do?" Walker asked.

I shrugged. "There was this sound. I can't describe it. It was like no sound you ever heard in your life." I pretended to shiver.

"Wow!" Darrell cried. He'd been attacking his potato salad like it might run away. But now he set down his fork. "Did you tell Scott?"

I shook my head. "Not yet. I think it's better to just be quiet about it until we know for sure. No sense making this ghost any madder than he already is."

"He's mad?" Eddie asked. His eyes widened.

I looked at Zack again. I wasn't too crazy about this part of our idea. "Well, sort of. I mean, you know. Ghosts are—uh—ghosts. They do scary stuff because they aren't happy. This one used to be a basketball player. Only he got killed the night before he was supposed to go to the NBA."

I breathed a sigh of relief when Scott interrupted. He announced that anyone needing costumes or music for the Talent Show could go to the storage room in the dining hall building and make their choices.

Lights out came at 10:30 P.M. sharp. I lay tense and waiting in my top bunk, staring out the window. Zack and I had decided to let the first tape finish before I went out and put ours in. That way we had a better chance of not being heard by anyone lying awake. The minutes crawled by slower than a lazy turtle in the middle of the highway. *Maybe there was no other tape*, I thought. *Maybe when the owner of the tape recorder went outside and found the first tape missing he decided not to take any more chances.* But then....

Rattle.

Rattle.

Clink.

Clank.

Below me, I heard Zack snort. I grinned. Chains were a little old. Compared to what was going to happen, they were about as scary as a mouse. When the rattling and clanking finally stopped, I crawled out from under the sheet and slid down the side of my bunk. Except for a few snores and sighs, the cabin was silent. I tiptoed to the door and out to the porch, shivering with excitement. I didn't even feel the stones and roots digging into my feet as I zipped around the side of the building. The recorder still sat on the knoll where we'd left it. I shined my flashlight on it and hit the stop button. The click seemed loud enough to wake up the whole camp. I moved fast, switched the tapes, and hurried back inside.

It took forever to start. My heart pounded. My hands got sweaty. I felt like I could jump out of my skin. And then ...

"AHHHHHHHHHHHHHH!" A scream sliced through the silence like the silver blade of a sharp sword.

The sound made me jump. I hadn't meant to turn it up quite that loud. We sounded good though. Really good. Like maybe we could do sound effects for Hollywood if the NBA didn't work out.

"WAAAAAAAA-LKER AAAAAAAA-DAMS!" That was me sounding as low and rumbly as far-off thunder.

Heads shot up off pillows. One guy yowled. Walker made a noise that sounded like he was strangling.

"M-m-m-m-m-m-ickeeeee!" he called.

I didn't answer. Another scream sailed through the window screen. And then an eerie whistle. Just when I thought I'd explode from the wonderfulness of it, the lights came on. I blinked and sat up.

"Okay, what's going on in here?" Scott demanded. The screen door slammed behind him. "This is the second time I've had to come over here this week!"

I hadn't planned on the tape waking up Scott. Outside the voice kept screaming and calling Walker's name.

"It's the Ghost of Camp Bee-a-Champ!" Walker cried. "It's after me!" He jumped down off his bunk and backed as far as he could away from the window.

"WHAT?" Scott bellowed. "There's no Ghost of Camp Bee-a-Champ! What's that racket out there?"

Everyone stopped screaming. I covered my

face with my hands and prayed for a spaceship to pull up outside the window. I'd rather be transported to Mars by little green guys than sit on my bunk listening to me and Zack moan and screech from the grassy knoll outside the window. With the lights on, we sounded about as scary as the Fun House at the first grade carnival.

"Mickey! That's YOU!" Eddie Parenti cried. "Now I know why you told us about the Ghost of Camp Bee-a-Champ! What's the big idea?"

"Yeah! What's the big idea?" Darrell demanded.

I looked down at Zack who had buried his head in his knees and refused to look at anybody. I guessed there wouldn't be any career in sound effects for us after all.

"I..." I looked over at Walker. "It's all his fault!" I blurted. "He started it. It's his tape recorder!"

Scott went over to where Walker was standing flat against the wall. "Is that true?" he asked.

Walked nodded. "It is my tape recorder," he agreed in a shaky voice. "And I was the one who turned it on every night. But the tapes aren't mine. Honest!"

9

Too Much Moaning
and Groaning

"So whose are they then?" I demanded. Now that Scott was looking at Walker instead of me, I felt much braver.

"I can't tell you," Walker said. "But don't be mad, Mickey. It was just for fun. And—and the person who did it really likes you."

I considered that. If Walker and Sam hadn't made the tapes, then there was only one possible person who knew me well enough to have gone to so much trouble—Tony Anzaldi. It seemed a little weird, though. Tony doesn't usually do stuff like that. But there was nobody else it could be. By the time Scott turned out the lights and warned us to settle down, I was convinced.

"Hey, Tony," I said at breakfast the next morning, "that was a good trick you pulled on me. I never figured out it was you until last night."

Tony looked at me blankly. "What trick was that?" he asked.

"You know—the scary noises. The ghost."

"I thought you were the one who pulled the ghost trick, Mick. It's all over camp." Tony picked up a carton of milk, opened it, and stuck in a plastic straw. "I'm confused."

I was confused too. If Tony hadn't done it, then who had? This was getting crazy!

At the gym, the coach from one of the local high schools ran us through our morning drills.

"Good, Mickey!" he yelled when I drove Zack out of my path to make a clean break for the basket. My shot hit the backboard and slammed through the hoop. The coach blew his whistle and stopped the play. "Do you know what you just did?" he asked me.

Sure—I'd landed myself a sweet one. But anybody could see that. I shook my head no.

"You used your feet to drive off the defender." He turned to the rest of the guys. "Footwork is something we think about for boxers. We forget it is equally important in basketball," he explained. "What Mickey did was called a jab step. He took a step right at the defender's outside foot. That should have forced him to react, but in this case it didn't. So Mickey took another step. That first step not only kept Zack back, but it also put Mickey in a position to shoot. Then his second step drove him closer to the basket."

Wow. I did all that and never even knew it! Suddenly I was a little sorry camp was almost over. All morning the same coach drilled us. Every time I came out on the court, he found something else he liked about my footwork.

"Good Mickey! Yes! Yes! Slide your feet when you defend. That's right! Yes, always bend at the knees, not the waist!"

"Wow, Mick, you were awesome today," Zack congratulated me on the way back to the cabin after practice. "I sure was the pits, wasn't I? But there's no sense moaning and groaning about it, I guess. Some days are like that."

I looked at Zack sharply. Moaning and groaning? A wild idea lit up my brain cells. Could it be ZACK who'd made the scary tapes and put Walker up to turning them on? Could Zack have played along with me so I wouldn't get suspicious? It sounded pretty weird, but it was the only possible answer. I was out of suspects.

"Yeah, we've sure had enough moaning and groaning going on around here," I answered. I picked up a stick and swung it around in the bushes like what I was saying was no big deal.

"That's for sure!" Zack frowned. "But you still don't know who tricked you, do you?"

I took a swing at a patch of thick weeds. "Oh,

I have an idea," I replied. "All that moaning and groaning kind of gave it away."

"Really?" Zack looked surprised. "I thought you didn't recognize any voices. I sure didn't, and I listened really hard."

I shrugged. "That's the thing with moaning and groaning," I answered. "It's tricky."

Zack gave me a weird look. "It sure is," he agreed. "That's why I was surprised Eddie Parenti knew it was you on our tape. Mostly you can't tell."

My heart raced. "True," I said. "But some moaning and groaning is just easy when you think about it."

Zack gave me another weird look. "Why do you keep saying that?" he asked in a cranky voice. "You must have said moaning and groaning six times in a row." He stopped in his tracks and stared at me. "You don't think it was ME do you?"

I kept walking. That's exactly what I thought. And I was getting surer of it by the second.

"That's crazy!" Zack cried, running after me. "Do you know how crazy that is? That's so crazy ..." He sputtered, trying to think of how crazy it was. "Well, it's just crazy, that's all."

We walked into the cabin just as Scott was

passing out mail. "Hey, guys!" he greeted us. "Mail for both of you." He tossed Zack a letter from his dad and handed me what was left.

One letter.

In a pink and purple envelope.

With a big sticker of a smiley face on the flap.

I looked around for Walker and saw him sitting on his bunk. No way was I going over to my own bunk to read a third letter from Trish Riley. I stood where I was and tore it open.

"Mick, that is a way crazy idea," Zack said again. "I did not play a trick on you! There is no way I ..." He gave up when he saw how interested I was in my letter and walked over to his bed to read his own mail. Out of the corner of my eye, I could see his face. It was redder than a fire hydrant. Good! Let him sweat a little, I thought. I unfolded the pink paper.

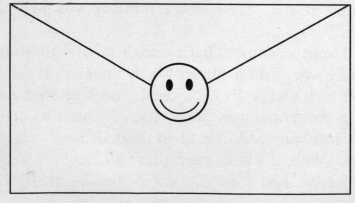

Dear Mickey,

How are you now? I am over my poison ivy. Almost. At least it doesn't ooze gunk any more. Now I have a bad sunburn. Yes, I really do. That's because I went swimming with Brittany at Lake Erie. We went to the water park at Cedar Point.

Have you been having fun? Brittany says to tell you that the best way to get rid of ghosts is to scare them back. But I think you should plug your ears if you hear any. You shouldn't listen too hard. It only makes them worse.

Oh! Did I say I miss you? Well, I do. When you come home my mom says you can come with us to the Cleveland Zoo. Say you will, OK?

From,

Trish

I finished reading the letter and started to fold it up.

"Hey Mick!" Walker called from his bunk "What did you get today?"

"Nothing!" I hollered back. I shoved the letter and the envelope in the pocket of my shorts. "Did you get any mail?"

He jumped down off his bunk and came over. "Yep, from my Aunt Nancy again. How about you?"

I shrugged. *He must have a crush on Trish Riley even bigger than Texas*, I thought. *It must be as big as all of America!* I couldn't imagine what it would be like to feel all goofy like that. Zack went goofy over some girl named Shawna Fox earlier in the year. But he got over it when she told everybody he had Dumbo ears. I sure hoped it would never happen to me.

"The usual." I said, shrugging.

Walker nodded. "Trish again, huh? That girl has ghosts on the brain! Hey, Zack!" he hollered. "Wait up! I'll go to lunch with you. Wanna come with us, Mickey?"

"You go ahead," I replied. "I'll catch up in a second." I waited until they were out the door before I pulled the letter out of my pocket.

My heart raced like an engine in overdrive.

Walker didn't know it, but he'd just handed me what I'd been looking for. Quickly, I reread the part about not listening too hard to ghosts. Yesssssssss! There it was! In plain pink and purple. My ghost wasn't even at Camp Bee-a-Champ! She was at home enjoying the joke. She'd sent the tapes with Walker. And Walker had played them for her. That's why he was so interested in the letters. It wasn't because he had a crush on her. He read them because he wanted to know what she was telling me! I laughed right out loud. Trish didn't like Walker. She still liked me!

"Mickey?"

I looked up as Scott came in the door. The rest of the guys had already left for lunch. I figured he was hurrying me up.

"I know! I'm coming," I said. "Hey, guess what? I just solved the ghost mystery!" I grinned at him. "You won't believe this, but ..."

He wasn't smiling.

I stopped and stared at him.

"Mickey," he said softly. "I'm afraid I have some bad news, buddy."

10

The Show Must Go On

"Bad news? What kind of bad news?" My heart pounded.

"Your mom called and ..."

The truth landed like a punch to the pit of my stomach. Scott didn't have to tell me. I already knew what it was. "No!" I shouted at him. "It's not true!"

"Mickey, listen. Your mom said you can go home right now if you want. She'll come get you today. She wants you to call her. It's about your grandma. She ..."

"NO!" I clapped both hands over my ears. I didn't want to hear Scott say that word. I would NOT listen to that word.

Scott put his arm around my shoulder and pulled me against him. I could smell his sweat and the sour scent of old aftershave lotion. "Come on," he said, leading me to the door. "Let's go call your mom."

We went to the office behind the gym. Scott

dialed my home number and handed me the phone. My head reeled. There had to be some sort of mistake. My mom would clear it up. She'd tell me that Scott hadn't heard her right. She'd tell me that everything was fine and I should have a good time at camp. "Mom?" I said into the phone. "Mom, it's me!"

"Oh, Sweetheart," she said. My mother never calls me sweetheart. Never. So sweetheart said everything there was to say. It was true after all. Scott was right. Grandma McGhee was dead.

"Mickey?"

"What?" The word ripped out of me, harsh and angry.

"I know how hard this is for you." Mom's voice cracked, then got higher. "You and Grandma McGhee had such a special bond. But Honey, she's with God now. God took her home to heaven!"

"How do you know?" I asked, feeling that punch in the pit of my stomach.

My mom's voice got so soft I could barely hear her. "Mickey, do you remember the first song Grandma ever taught you to sing?" she asked.

Before I could answer she started to sing the words I knew by heart.

Jesus loves me, this I know,

For the Bible tells me so ...

By the time she got to the second verse, it was like hearing Grandma McGhee. I held the phone so tight my knuckles turned white. I closed my eyes and just listened.

Jesus loves me, He who died,
Heaven's gate to open wide;
He will wash away my sin,
Let His little child come in.

Then she stopped. The seconds ticked by as slow as waiting for the final buzzer when I've sunk the winning shot.

"That's how we know, Mickey," she said. "And you know what else? The wonderful part is that she's still with you too. And always will be. Forever."

"How can she be with me if she's with God?" I asked angrily. My voice sounded small and tinny, like I was talking through an old can.

"It's a hard thing to understand, I know," Mom answered. In my mind, I could see her sitting at the kitchen table, watching the tail of the cat clock swish back and forth as she talked. "But she'll be with you in a thousand ways you have yet to discover. All you have to do is taste lemonade. Or remember her playing music for you in the kitchen. Or remember those funny tilted cakes she used to make. And she'll be right there. Grandma lives with God. But a part of her lives on in your heart, Mickey. She'll stay as long as you need her to. I promise."

By the time I hung up the phone, I was crying. Mom was coming to get me. But not until tomorrow. At first I had wanted to go home right away. And then, all of a sudden, I didn't any more. I needed time alone before my family swallowed me up. All my Illinois cousins would be coming. Plus all the people in the neighborhood and all Grandma's friends from church.

"You want to go back to the cabin and lie down for a while?" Scott asked me when I hung up. "It's okay if you do."

I nodded. "I can go alone," I said. Suddenly I wanted him gone. I needed to talk to God. Ask Him if my mom was right. And if she was, ask Him to somehow show me so I'd know for sure. I scrubbed my face with my T-shirt and sniffed loudly. Scott clapped me on the back and let me go.

Outside, I could hear the wild shrieks of the guys swimming in the lake. I turned right, away from the water and noise, and walked down the quiet path to the cabin. Part of me felt like the news wasn't real. But the other part—the bigger part—knew it was.

Why God?

My feet kept time to the question. I must have asked it a million times before I reached the cabin and climbed up on my bunk. I lay there in the hot$ stuffy quiet, watching the chipmunks run up and down the pole of the birdfeeder, stuffing their tiny cheeks with seeds. I didn't know the answer to that question. She'd had a long life. I knew that. But why now? Why did it have to happen now when I wasn't there? I didn't know. After a while, though, I did know something else. It started like a tiny ping in my brain and grew and grew, until there was only one thing for me to do. I jumped up and ran down the path as fast as I could.

"Scott!" I yelled as soon as the lake came into sight. "Scott!"

"What is it, Mickey? You okay?" Scott flipped off of a blue raft and carried it to shore. He dropped it next to a black, rubber inner tube and ran toward me.

"I—need—to—ask you—something!" I panted. "Do you have any—music—you know—tapes or CDs or—anything?"

Scott scratched his head. "Sure. Back where we keep all the costumes and stuff for the Talent

Show there's an old record player and a ton of records. What do you need?" He looked surprised. But no more surprised than I was. This idea could only have come from one place. It sure didn't seem to be anything I'd decided on my own.

"I need something for tonight, for the Talent Show," I said, finally catching my breath. "But you might not have it. I really need it, Scott."

Scott scratched his head again when I told him what I wanted. "Wow. That's a tough one," he admitted. "Let's go see though."

The storage room behind the gym made me sneeze. All the records were old and dusty. Some were big and thin. Some were medium-sized and thick. And some were small with a hole in the middle like a doughnut. I looked through stacks. And stacks. And more stacks. And then I found it!

"I got it! Scott, I got it!" I screamed, jumping up and down. "Can we use this? Will it work?" I held out the heavy, medium-sized record.

Scott nodded. "It'll be pretty scratchy, but I think it will work."

I knew people might laugh at me. They might think it was a big joke. But I wasn't doing it for them. I was doing it for Grandma McGhee. And God. And me. And in a way, for my family too. It was a way to find out for myself if my mom was right. I hugged the dusty record to my chest and headed back to the cabin. I would still do the commercial with Zack, but I would also do the thing that always made my grandma laugh and clap her hands in the kitchen.

It was dark when the Talent Show began. The campfire cast a warm glow on the 105 faces gathered around it. Walker took the stage first with his Elvis song. It brought the whole crowd to its feet. We laughed and swayed until our sides ached—even mine. Sam Sherman sang a popular song with another guy from his cabin after that. They were terrific—of course. Sam is one of those perfect people who does everything great. He plays basketball great. He does math great. And now he sings great. Sometimes I don't think it's fair. But tonight it didn't matter one bit.

When he was done, Tony Anzaldi did a funny skit with the rest of the guys from their cabin about an invisible horse. Then Zack and I did our Taco Bell commercial, and I got to be the dog. My Mexican accent made Walker fall over sideways laughing. After that, a bunch of people we didn't know performed. One guy played the violin. Another one told jokes like a stand-up comic. And a bunch of them sang. Some were so bad it's a wonder the coyotes weren't howling at the moon. It wasn't until the very end that I took my turn on stage alone.

"We have one more performance," Scott said into the microphone. "Mickey McGhee is going to do something very special for us. Without a Mexican accent this time!"

Everybody laughed.

"I want you all to put your hands together one more time for our good friend Mickey!" Scott clapped loudly and everybody joined in. But I could tell that they were all looking at each other, confused.

Slowly I walked up the steps of the porch and faced the sea of faces around the fire. I held my body stiff and looked out over their heads. *Help me, God. Help them not to laugh. Help it be okay. And please God—please let Grandma know I'm doing this for her.*

I nodded to Scott and balled my hands into tight fists. The music started—scratchy and not too loud. It was okay, though. I knew that music like I knew the taste of my grandmother's lemonade. It was the same music that had swirled around her kitchen for as long as I could remember. I counted the beats in my head, stood up on my toes, and kicked out my right leg.

I danced the Irish jig.

And nobody laughed.

"Wow! Do you hear that clapping?" Walker asked when I jumped off the stage. "Man, you were a hit, Mick!"

I heard it. It sounded like thunder rolling through the woods. But the funny thing was I didn't care. I hadn't danced to be a star. Most of the time I want stardom more than anything. But not this time. This time I just wanted to do something special for my grandma. And feel her smile while she watched.

After the Talent Show, I walked back to the cabin with Zack and Walker.

"I didn't know you could dance, Mick!" Zack exclaimed. "How come you never told me?"

I shrugged. "It's just something my grandma taught me. It never came up I guess."

"Well, I think it's cool," Walker said.

"I'm sorry about your grandmother, Mick," Zack said. "I don't know what it feels like to have somebody die."

"I'm sorry too, "Walker added.

For a few seconds, nobody said anything. It felt weird—like I should be making them feel better instead of the other way around. But then Walker broke the silence.

"Hey, Mickey?"

"What?" I looked up at the sky. Tomorrow I would be home and the next day Walker and Zack would be too. I wondered what was happening at my house right now. Was my dad sad? Was he remembering Grandma and what it was like when he was my age and she was his mom? My dad doesn't show how he feels much. Not about stuff like that anyhow.

"You aren't mad at me about the ghost thing, are you? I really only helped. It wasn't my idea. Honest!"

"Hey, it's okay!" I answered, punching him lightly on the arm. "I know who did it."

"Who?" Zack asked. "It wasn't ME! I told you that already Mickey."

I laughed and punched him, too. "I know that. It was Trish. She's one seriously goofy girl."

"TRISH?" Zack shouted.

"Yep," Walker answered. "That's right. You guessed it, Mick." He ran a few yards ahead and pointed to a clearing in the trees. "Wow! Look over there! Let's go run around for a minute. Want to? There must be a zillion lightning bugs over there!"

Zack and I followed him through the long grass into the field. In the distance lay the lake, and farther off the horse barn. But mostly all you could see was open space and a wide sky dotted with stars. Everywhere I looked, fireflies twinkled like the lights of heaven. I spun around in a circle until I got so dizzy I fell over. Walker and Zack ran and screamed, but I lay there quietly, looking up at the sky. Mom was right about God—same as always. He'd taken my grandmother home. But He'd left part of her behind too—inside me. I looked over at my buddies and smiled as three fireflies blinked at the same time.